This book is dedicated to
Class 3 Year 1, 2006/7
St Nicolas Primary School, Abingdon

30 of the brightest stars!

With special thanks to
Anne Wattam
Sally Dougan

The idea for this book came about during a class visit to my daughter's school.
I asked the class for a list of characters so we could build a story around them,
and the first offering was A Star-Faced Crocodile. Amazing!
Soon, we had a cast, a plot (of sorts), and a funny feeling we were going to need more
than the remaining 20 minutes to finish it.

So began the journey. We wrote and illustrated the story. There was a poem, a song,
a play, even a sticky day making papier-mâché crocodiles, and more fun than I thought
possible with that many children!

What follows is an adaptation of all of the above. I hope it carries the same spirit,
energy and enthusiasm we all had throughout that memorable time.

The Star-Faced Crocodile
by David Melling

First published in 2008 by Hodder Children's Books

Text and illustrations copyright © David Melling 2008

Hodder Children's Books
338 Euston Road
London NW1 3BH

Hodder Children's Books Australia
Level 17/207 Kent Street
Sydney, NSW 2000

A catalogue record of this book is
available from the British Library.

ISBN: 978 0 340 93047 2

10 9 8 7 6 5 4 3

Printed in China

Hodder Children's Books
is a division of Hachette
Children's Books
An Hachette UK Company

www.hachette.co.uk

THE
STAR-FACED
CROCODILE

DAVID MELLING

Hodder
Children's
Books

A division of Hachette Children's Books

ONE NIGHT A BEAR SETTLED DOWN
BY THE EDGE OF A LAKE AND SANG
TO THE STARS THAT DANCED AND
PLAYED IN THE WATER.

A shy crocodile, drifting by, had never
heard such a beautiful song and he
swished his long tail in time
to the music.

'Oh my!'
gasped the bear...

'A STAR-FACED CROCODILE!'

The bear was happy to see such a wonderful creature!
He sang every night, and every night he asked
the crocodile to dance.
The crocodile wanted to so much, but he was afraid
to come out of the lake. 'If I do,' he sighed,
'he'll see I'm just a plain, ordinary,
snippy-snappy crocodile!'
It's not easy making
friends when you
have so many teeth.

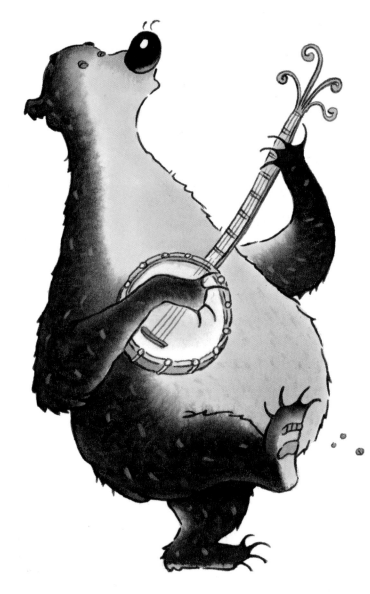

Then the crocodile had an idea. He made a tall hat from some white star-flowers that were growing nearby.

He crept closer to the singing bear and, when he felt brave enough, he stepped out and started to dance.

But as he danced the petals

fell

out,

one

by

one . . .

'Oh flip!' said the crocodile. He dashed back to the lake
and slipped quietly into the water.

The bear could see he was indeed just an ordinary
crocodile, but he didn't mind.

'Wait!' he called, 'don't go!'

The crocodile didn't hear him.

The bear missed the crocodile and his toothy smile.
He whispered to the dozy trees, 'I think my friend wants to look
like a star-faced crocodile. Can you help?'

The trees yawned and stretched out their long arms . . . until there were no stars left in the sky!

'Look at our pretty twinkles!' said the trees.

They were so dazzled by the stars they decided to keep them for themselves.

But the crocodile had other ideas.

The crocodile swam down, down, down to the very bottom of the lake. With no starlight and an empty sky, the forest was plunged into an eerie darkness.

Oh how dark it was!
The moon was worried
the trees might take her
as well, so she hid
behind a cloud.
The bear and the
trees had a funny
feeling they had
all made a mistake.
'I'll play a tune
to cheer us up,' said the bear.

'Snap!' went a string.

'Oh!' said the trees.

'Bother!' said the bear.

Meanwhile, the crocodile
was finally ready to show everyone
how splendid he looked.
But nobody noticed and, besides,
the stars had lost their twinkle.

Suddenly he felt very silly.

It was very quiet. There was no light, no music and no dancing. They all realised that if the stars disappeared

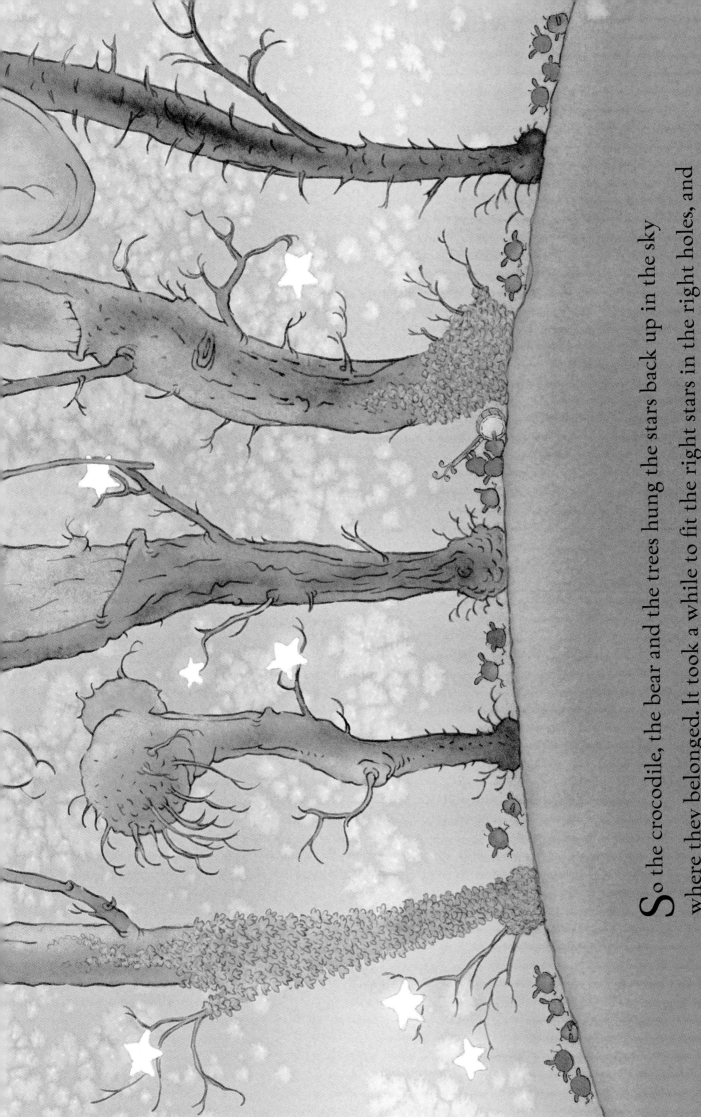

So the crocodile, the bear and the trees hung the stars back up in the sky where they belonged. It took a while to fit the right stars in the right holes, and the hooks were quite fiddly, but it was worth it in the end.

'Look,' said the crocodile with a toothy grin, 'they've got their twinkle back!'

Starlight returned to the forest at last. Before long,
so did the moon and the music and the dancing.
Then a shooting star fell from the sky and landed
in the lake, right next to the crocodile.
The water glowed and fizzled and,
after a moment, there he was . . .

...a Star-Faced Crocodile!

Or was it just a trick of the light?